The Old Woman and Her Pig

illustrated by
W. T. MARS

Once upon a time a poor old woman lived alone in a little house. One day as she was sweeping her floor, she found a shiny sixpence.

"Oh, my!" she said. "How lucky I am! Now I can buy a nice fat pig."

The old woman put on her bonnet and went to the market and there she bought a fat pig.

She was very happy as she started home with her pig. But when they came to a stile over a stone wall, the pig would not go over the stile.

The old woman
tried to pull
the pig.

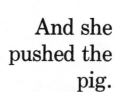

And she
pushed the
pig.

And she scolded
the pig. But the
pig would not go
over the stile.

"Oh! What shall I do?" said the old woman. "If the pig will not go over the stile, I shall not get home tonight."

The old woman went back the way she had come, hoping to find someone to help her.

Soon she met a dog. She said to the
dog:

"Dog, dog, bite my pig. Pig will not go
over the stile. And I shall not get home
tonight."

But the dog would not bite the pig.

The old woman went on until she met
a stick. She said to the stick:

"Stick, stick, beat the dog. Dog will
not bite my pig. Pig will not go over the
stile. And I shall not get home tonight."

But the stick would not beat the dog.

Soon the old woman saw a fire. She said to the fire:

"Fire, fire, burn the stick. Stick will not beat the dog.

"Dog will not bite my pig. Pig will not go over the stile. And I shall not get home tonight."

But the fire would not burn the stick.

By and by the old woman came to some water. She said to the water:

"Water, water, put out the fire. Fire will not burn the stick. Stick will not beat the dog.

"Dog will not bite my pig. Pig will not go over the stile. And I shall not get home tonight."

But the water would not put out the fire.

The old woman went on until she met an ox. She said to the ox:

"Ox, ox, drink the water. Water will not put out the fire.

"Fire will not burn the stick. Stick will not beat the dog. Dog will not bite my pig. Pig will not go over the stile. And I shall not get home tonight."

But the ox would not drink the water.

By this time the old woman was very angry. So, when she met the butcher, she said to him:

"Butcher, butcher, kill the ox. Ox will not drink the water. Water will not put out the fire.

"Fire will not burn the stick. Stick will not beat the dog. Dog will not bite my pig. Pig will not go over the stile. And I shall not get home tonight."

But the butcher would not kill the ox.

The old woman looked up and saw a long rope hanging from a tree. She said to the rope:

"Rope, rope, tie up the butcher. Butcher will not kill the ox. Ox will not drink the water.

"Water will not put out the fire. Fire will not burn the stick. Stick will not beat the dog. Dog will not bite my pig. Pig will not go over the stile. And I shall not get home tonight."

But the rope would not tie up the butcher.

The poor old woman sat down to rest. "Oh, if only someone would help me," she said aloud.

Just then she heard a noise. She looked around and saw a little mouse.

"What can I do to help?" asked the mouse.

The old woman was glad to find a
friend. She said to the mouse:

"Mouse, mouse, gnaw the rope. Rope
will not tie up the butcher. Butcher will
not kill the ox. Ox will not drink the
water. Water will not put out the fire.
Fire will not burn the stick.

"Stick will not beat the dog. Dog will not bite my pig. Pig will not go over the stile. And I shall not get home tonight."

"That I will," said the mouse. And —

the mouse
began to gnaw
the rope. The
rope began to
tie up the
butcher. The
butcher began
to kill the ox.
The ox began to
drink the water.

The water began to put out the fire. The fire began to burn the stick. The stick began to beat the dog.

The dog began to bite the pig. The pig gave a great big jump.

He jumped right over the stile and —

the old woman really did get home that night.